P9-EKY-762

For my dear friend
Pauline Wood Steiman
with love
Waboose

For Olivia Weinstock,
and for Reuben and Livya
Maimon, from their friend
on the other side of the
ocean — LR

Text copyright © 2014 by Martha Brooks
Illustrations copyright © 2014 by Leticia Ruifernández
Published in Canada and the USA in 2014 by Groundwood Books

Groundwood Books / House of Anansi Press
110 Spadina Avenue, Suite 801, Toronto, Ontario M5V 2K4
or c/o Publishers Group West
1700 Fourth Street, Berkeley, CA 94710

We acknowledge for their financial support of our publishing program the
Canada Council for the Arts, the Government of Canada through the Canada
Book Fund (CBF) and the Ontario Arts Council.

Library and Archives Canada Cataloguing in Publication
Brooks, Martha, author
Winter moon song / by Martha Brooks ; illustrated by Leticia
Ruifernández.
Issued in print and electronic formats.
ISBN 978-1-55498-320-9 (bound).—ISBN 978-1-55498-321-6 (pdf)
I. Ruifernández, Leticia, illustrator II. Title.
PS8553.R663W55 2014   jC813'.54   C2014-900884-8
C2014-900885-6

The illustrations were done in watercolor and ink.
Design by Michael Solomon
Printed and bound in Malaysia

Winter Moon Song

MARTHA BROOKS

PICTURES BY

LETICIA RUIFERNÁNDEZ

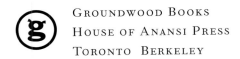

GROUNDWOOD BOOKS

HOUSE OF ANANSI PRESS

TORONTO BERKELEY

ONCE UPON A TIME, in the far deep woods, when the snow looked as if a giant hand had tossed a blanket of stars to earth, there lived a rabbit. He was a youngish rabbit, not so small as to be a still-doted-upon baby, yet not big enough to be noticed in any significant way. He loved to sing — not by himself, but he was learning to do so, quite confidently, with others.

The wind ruffled his ears as he made his way home from choir practice. Their last rehearsal had gone pretty well, and the ancient, difficult but thrilling piece of music called "Winter Moon Song" was as ready as it was going to be.

Tomorrow evening, rabbits would come from everywhere to hear the song performed in grand tradition, inside the gathering place with its majestic windows and the fingering trees beyond.

As they had done since the beginning, every few years new singers replaced the old ones — rabbits who had lost their voices or could no longer remember the song and who, in either case, sank into the background, mumbling the odd note.

The rabbit, a new singer, stopped in the snow to think about this. Then, turning his round eyes to the round moon, he tilted his head curiously. There it was in all its mysterious beauty — the pattern of a rabbit on the moon.

For the first time in his life, he thought about how all the old singers were once young like him, looking at that rabbit, every one of them asking their mothers the same question — "How did it get there? How did that rabbit get there?"

"It's a tricky story," his own mother had answered.

"Does it have a happy ending?"

"It isn't happy or sad," she said. "It just is."

"Can you tell it to me?"

"Ah, yes. A long, long time ago, our Great Mother, Creator Rabbit, came to earth," his mother began. "She wanted to see how it felt to be one of her creations. Soon she found it was a lonely business, not at all what she expected. She wandered around, cold and confused and hungry. She built a fire and put a stewpot of snow over the flames to melt, and there she stood shivering, watching as the snow turned to bubbling water. 'I must have been crazy,' she said, 'to think that this would be a nice place for all of them I love so dearly.'

"As she stood there, a little rabbit who was not too big and not too small came hopping by. He said to himself, 'That's my Great Mother, Creator Rabbit. I must save her or she will die!' With that he jumped into the stewpot.

"'Oh no, I must save my creation or he will die!'
cried the Great Rabbit, as she reached into the pot,
grabbed him up by the ears and flung him at the moon."

The rabbit's own mother paused and pointed to the place where the rabbit had landed.

"And there he is to this day," she continued. "That's why we call him the rabbit-in-the-moon."

"But what about Great Mother Rabbit?"

"She went back to the place she came from."

"That's it?" he said.

"That's it," replied his mother. "Except, of course, that's why we sing 'Winter Moon Song.' To lighten the darkest month of the year with a trail of magic. Do you like that idea?"

He answered her with a smile that was neither big nor small, but was more like a question in the middle of things.

And now he turned up his face one more time
and said goodnight to the rabbit-in-the-moon.

He turned once again, disappearing through
the opening of his burrow. There, tucking his
paws under his silvery-white body, he settled on a
bed of cedar boughs.

Through the hole of the burrow he could still
see the moon. A question slowly formed in his
mind. The more he thought, the more he felt
certain that it was an important question. Maybe
no one had ever thought such a thing before. The
idea that he might be the first such rabbit sent
shivers of rapture through his body. The question
itself filled his whole spirit as, finally, he slept.

The next evening, rabbits from near and far began to fill the space where "Winter Moon Song" would be performed. The rabbit took his own place with the choir. There they all waited as everyone who had come to hear them shuffled and whispered and coughed below, and the last of the old ones found their places.

The gleaming windows shut out the night. Candles flickered everywhere. The choir poised on one breath. The age-old song began. And when, one hour later, the audience applauded and nudged the old ones awake and then headed happily for the door, the song was done again for another year.

A throng of rabbits poured out into the wintry air. The little rabbit stood among them as they visited and chattered and gossiped. Some of them even said that they found the choir particularly stirring this year — such lovely voices!

But he was not convinced. It had been beautiful, yes — even thrilling — but it hadn't been, as his mother described, a magical path lighting the darkest month. The winter moon hung above them, the rabbit pattern clearly visible. Nobody seemed to notice.

Softly, in the middle of everything, he began to hum the ancient song. And then, as no one appeared to be listening, he sang it a little louder.

An old rabbit standing nearby turned slowly and said, "Now, isn't that nice. Do you remember the whole thing?"

The young rabbit stopped singing and nodded solemnly.

"Well, then, laddie," cried the elder, "start from the beginning — and don't leave out a single note!"

The rabbit felt a flicker of panic.

"The first note," the elder prompted. "What is it?"

"It's a breath, first. We all have to take a breath, and, and … to think about it. That's how we begin."

"Very good, then, take your breath."

"Now?"

"Yes."

"Oh my," said the rabbit.

Bravely, he began. He took the first breath, alone. He sang the first note, alone — a note that was long and very beautiful and the reason, too, for such a deep breath — a single note that made everyone listen.

The elder sighed. A tear rolled down his face and fell into the snow at his feet.

Some of the rabbits had already hopped away to their homes. But many remained, young and old and everything in between, and now all of them listened intently to "Winter Moon Song," sung, as the young rabbit felt it should be, under the winter moon.

Some joined in. Several old ones, including the elder, found their voices — voices that had been lost over time — and they sang with a youthful lusty joy. And when the song was over and everyone gazed up at the rabbit-in-the-moon, they all felt that they were not separate or lonely but part of one great rabbit family.

"This was the best night ever," the rabbit said to his mother, who had stayed around to hear him sing and create a new tradition. Together, then, they made their way home in the crisp night air as snow fell like stars all around them.

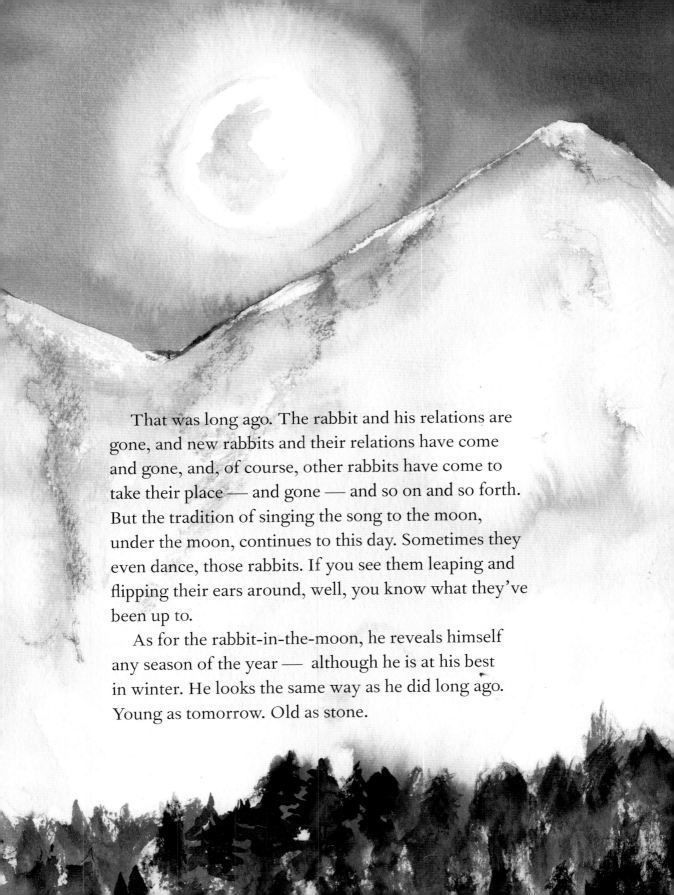

That was long ago. The rabbit and his relations are gone, and new rabbits and their relations have come and gone, and, of course, other rabbits have come to take their place — and gone — and so on and so forth. But the tradition of singing the song to the moon, under the moon, continues to this day. Sometimes they even dance, those rabbits. If you see them leaping and flipping their ears around, well, you know what they've been up to.

As for the rabbit-in-the-moon, he reveals himself any season of the year — although he is at his best in winter. He looks the same way as he did long ago. Young as tomorrow. Old as stone.

VARIOUS FORMS OF MOON RABBIT creation tales pop up in
storytelling cultures throughout the world. They feature in the
folklore of China, Korea and Japan. A Buddhist tale tells of an old
man begging for food. A monkey offers him fruit, an otter offers
fish, a jackal, stolen food. Finally, a rabbit, who has nothing to offer
but the grass it eats, sacrifices itself by leaping into the old man's
fire. The rabbit survives, and the old man, who is really Sakka, the
ruler of Heaven, rewards the rabbit for its goodness by painting its
image on the moon.

Variations of the Moon Rabbit story appear on this continent,
in Aztec and Cree cultures, among others. Bobby Woods —
Lakota Elder and Sweat Lodge leader — shared one such story, or
teaching, with me outside a truck on a cold, crisp moon-filled night
at Cross Lake, Manitoba. I am a singer and had given him the gift
of song, a sweet balm for his insomnia, and he kindly returned the
magic. I've reconfigured that teaching, setting it at the center of my
own story. The difference is that I imagined a female deity — Great
Mother, Creator Rabbit — and then swirling around that central
story is my own story of the little rabbit who dares to break with
tradition and create his own honoring of the moon.

— Martha Brooks

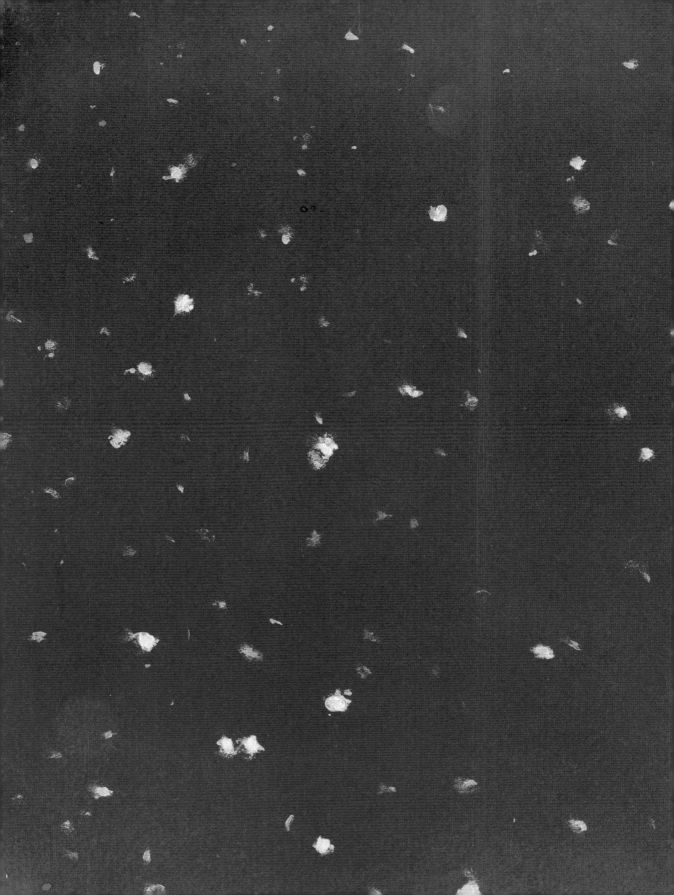